Lochnagar

Ruthven's Revenge

And Other Metrical Tales

Lochnagar

Ruthven's Revenge
And Other Metrical Tales

ISBN/EAN: 9783337074074

Printed in Europe, USA, Canada, Australia, Japan

Cover: Foto ©Andreas Hilbeck / pixelio.de

More available books at **www.hansebooks.com**

RUTHVEN'S REVENGE

AND

Other Metrical Tales.

BY

LOCHNAGAR,

Edinburgh:

MACLACHLAN AND STEWART.

1862.

Contents.

Ruthven's Revenge.

I.

Y lofty crags which ftem the tide
That rolls to Scotia's weftern fide:
Crags which conceal the dreary cave
Where oft the noble and the brave,
By every hope difown'd,
As war protracted fed diftrefs,
And left no fhadow of fuccefs,
Secure afylum found.
Here, too, ftill fertile in her ftore
Of themes, traditionary lore
Speaks of a beaming fpectred light,
Which floods the difmal cell by night—
Tells that the Demon of the Storm
Sometimes difplays his awful form;

Charging the elements to rife,
And battle with the fea and fkies.

II.

Nor this alone : of raptured love,
    In female grace difplay'd,
Through hoftile ages fhe hath ftrove
    To fpeak of Gayford's maid.
Here virtue lent her every charm
Which can the female paffions warm ;
In air and manner dignified,
She her companions far outvied :
How mufical her mellow voice,
    That deep impreffion made
On the glad objeƈt of her choice,
    As he his amours paid !
Beauty her imprefs fure might trace
Upon her well-proportion'd face :
Expreffive were her azure eyes,
    And foft the fmile that from her fell :
Nobly her forehead feem'd to rife—
    Told where intelligence did dwell :
Still gently o'er her lovely neck
    The auburn hair in ringlets lay.
    O ! where the youth, fond reader fay,
Who would not fight for Mary's fake !

III.

She was an only daughter, and
Her charms were prized throughout the land.
Though of a noble family fprung,
    In whofe veins flow'd the Norman blood—
A race by ancient poets sung,
    By conquering William's fide they ftood.
Who has not heard Montgomery's name?—
Still Wales and Ayr refound his fame.
Her branch had felt ftern fortune's rage,
And loft its wide-ftretch'd heritage—
A minor fragment now remain'd
To her of all her fathers gain'd.
One grateful parent was no more,
    He fell at Bothwell's dreadful fight;
The fecond Charles' arms he bore,
    And died in gallant Monmouth's fight.
In Gayford's cottage on the bafe
Of that rude crag where Aufter plays,
In cherifh'd folitude ftill ftay'd
The mother of the beauteous maid.

IV.

There rolls a clear but noify rill,
    Which Gayford's northern fide adorns;

It takes its courſe from yonder hill,
  And by the tower of Craighall turns.
The angler, at approach of noon,
  Here lonely may be ſeen;
And often has the horn'd moon
  'Held Mary on the green.
In flowing robe ſhe walk'd alone
From Gayford to the Angler's Stone.
But hark! a light ſtep greets the ear,—
  Fair Mary knows its ſound:
Her darling William doth appear,
  And to her arms doth bound!
What higher joy can heav'n above
  On human kind beſtow,
Than lend its ſmile in bluſhing love,
  Which ſtills the jeer of woe!

v.

The handſome form of William Graham
  Scarce twenty winters' ſnows had ſeen;
Vigorous was his hardy frame,
  Striking his hazel eyeballs' gleam!
Pure was his love-entranced heart,
  Vermilion was his laughing cheek!
Here alſo Knowledge ſeem'd to ſtart,
  And William for her model ſeek!

He, as a thinker, in the ſhade
   Caſt many of maturer years;
Moral Philoſophy, 'tis ſaid,
A favourite ſtudy he had made;
   Loved he the grave and learned ſeers.
Oft on the page of hiſtory
The noble youth had caſt his eye;
Admired he each bold Spartan ſire—
   Admired he the Athenian ſage!
O'erjoy'd to mark the Roman fire,
   And Hannibal's vindictive rage;
Or Marcus Brutus raiſe the knife
   That ſnatch'd the imperial deſpot's life.
And, like each patriot Scottiſh ſon,
   The name of Wallace ſtirr'd his blood;
He heard how Stirling bridge was won,
   And England's warriors ſwell'd the flood.
But chief admired the glorious field
   Where Scotland ſaw her fortunes turn—
Saw England's hundred thouſand yield
   At the immortal Bannockburn!
Still, William oft on ſtate affairs
   His prized, his leiſure moments ſpent,
   Muſing, as o'er the plains he went,
How Alfred father'd England's cares,
Conquering the mighty Danes that braved the land;

Maintaining juftice with an able hand!
He loved the principle the Charter gave,
    And forth as freedom's champion ftood;
    Yet many of the points he would,
On gen'rous thought and reafon, waive.
Science was then in infancy.
The rapturous fwell of poefy
Recall'd his love of other days:
    Himfelf a poet was,
And in foul-ftirring magic lays
    Upheld the glorious caufe
Of liberty of confcience—and
Religious freedom in the land!

VI.

Such is our hero: fuch the fon
    And heir of valiant Henry Graham,
The knight whofe prowefs great him won
    In Flemifh fight a deathlefs name!
Supported he Blake's mighty wars,
And fpoke indignant of the fcars
The fire of furious Holland gave,
When dark deftruction fwept the wave.
Though of a branch of famed Montrofe,
    In youth he Cromwell's caufe upheld;
An en'my was to Claverhoufe—

Rejoiced he o'er the gory field
That laid the victor-hero dead—
(Ah! then the hopes of Stuart fled!)
Craighall was his, whofe feudal fway
Three hundred vaffals did obey.

VII.

" But, William," fmiling, Mary faid,
 As on his breaft her head fhe laid,
" What forrows prey upon thy mind?
 Shall galling recollections dare
To type upon thy forehead care—
 Alas! in thee a victim find?"
" My father, ah!" was the reply—
Was follow'd fwiftly by a figh;
His throbbing bofom fcarce could tell
The fource from which thefe forrows fell.
" Enough," confufed, his Mary faid—
 " Enough, too well the reft I know;
The unfeeling wretch fome fcheme hath laid—
 Wretch! caufe of fair Montgomery's woe:
Alas, alas! thy father hears
 This plot for our deftruction laid,
I guefs;" and here the falling tears
 A while her fad narration ftay'd.
" Alas that ere my charms begat,

Ruthven, in thee a fuitor keen;
From the beginning well you knew
    I ne'er could give my love to you.
All thy falfe ways did Mary fpurn,
That her intentions thou mightſt learn—
    Since this negleƈt, knave, thou haſt fet
On dire deſtruƈtion : have I been,
    Have I, and muſt I—muſt I yet
Bend low to thy relentlefs fpleen ?"

VIII.

She faid; and in a fwoon ſhe fell
    While refting on her William's breaſt.
And while on her ſharp anguiſh ſtole,
Array'd with fell defpondency,
He ſtrove to foothe her agony,
    And fet her wayward fears to reſt :
Her wonted fpirits 'gan to rife—
    Her rapid fancy gleam'd again;
Catching a glance of William's eyes,
    She rofe revigor'd from the pain—
An hour flaſh'd by : the echo yet
    Of gentle whifpers might be caught—
Embraces with embraces met,
    With cheerful Heaven's applaufes fraught—
Laugh quickly met with amorous fmile,

And time feem'd fhort the happy while—
Lips met with lips—a parting fign!
    Our hero's anxious father waits
The arrival of his worthy fon,
    Who ftill with Gayford's Mary prates:
" When Night has hufh'd the twilight's reign,
    And fpread her ftillnefs o'er the plain,
By Craighall's woody knoll shall I
    To-morrow wait for thee:
O that the bleffed hour fped nigh!
O fad—how fad—it is to leave
The one to whom my heart doth cleave!
But it muft be: my father's found
Already rings his hall around—
    That mighty found for me!"

                    IX.

The lovers part: our hero takes
    The antique road to green Craighall;
On either fide the giant brakes
    High overlook the heavy wall.
Here oft hath antiquarian ftrove
To point the dark, the facred grove,
    Where Druids kept the fpoils of war.
Here, glancing o'er the lofty trees,
A tower'd cairn the ftranger fees,

Where oft the infants' rending cries
Were heard at Druids' facrifice:
The tranfmigration of the foul
  To bright or gloomy regions far,
    The fathers taught with fome regard.
    Their feeble voice the Britons heard—
    The infamy on fceptic paft,
    The fneers at every doubter caft,
Awhile fuperior reafon ftole.
Now onward, and he gains the well
  Where fairy elves, 'tis faid,
Met with a modeft, beauteous belle,
  Come by the eaftern glade.
They carried her to Fairyland,
  Its pleafant fights to view;
Admired fhe Queen of Elfins' wand:
Again fhe came to earth transform'd,
And many a gallant fquire deform'd
  She once as fuitor knew!
And now a rivulet he gains
  That tells its tragic tale;
Here lufty Robert of the Mains
  In duel boldly fell—
And here the Wizard's ruftling oak
Climbs o'er the bofom of a rock.

X.

Ah ! how uncouth our hero's mood,
While pacing through the lonely wood
That by the manfion grew,
   In fober, deep foliloquy,
The paft he did review,
   And fancied dark futurity.
" What monfter lies are often form'd
   To fcoff at fallen greatnefs ! Ah !
How oft is cruel deed perform'd,
   And yet th' offender braves the law !
Oh ! that I faw this daftard bleed,
And pay the forfeit of his deed ?
That juftice would his name difgrace,
And ftamp with infamy his race—
That race ignoble, prone to crime,
That thrice difhonour'd hath our time !

XI.

" Full oft hath dang'rous Ruthven told
(That man fo oft to perjury fold !)
My father lies of Mary's worth—
A fairer gem ne'er deck'd the north !
He, prone fuch ftories to fuftain,
   Frowns bitterly upon his fon—

Yet all thefe frowns on me are vain!
He from the firft difdain'd this maid,
Becaufe her fire gave Stuart aid
   Before his crown he won.
In pomp and wealth my father rolls,
In Spanifh and in Fleming fpoils;
And overlooks the fading name
   Of once renown'd Montgomery:
And yet, how true this very fame
   Prefents the higheft charm to me!
Mean is the man who dares to fmile,
While frowning fate triumphs the while:
Expand thy weapons, jealoufy,
That worth and gentlenefs would ftain,
For manhood doth them now difdain.
Ruthven, if yet within my reach
   You ere fhould chance to ftray,
Direful the leffon I will teach
   Thee, coward, of thy way!
Father, I nobly thee forgive;
   Yet pity thou art led
With faithful William thus to ftrive,
   And accept Ruthven's aid.
The time fhall come when thou fhalt fee,
   And pity, ah! my wrong;
For gen'rous thou haft been to me,

Except in this alone.
And oh! my Mary, I rejoice
    To think thy wonted fpirits rose,
Even when fail'd my faltering voice
    To warn thee of approaching woes.
O! may my prefence ere infpire
    Thy pure, thy rapturous heart with joy;
And never fure fhall forrow dire
    Thy fofter feelings e'er annoy."

XII.

Young Graham hath gain'd the lofty hall:
    In front a maffive pillar fhone;
And topp'd upon that column tall,
    A hero's image rofe from ftone.
That hero was the poet-king,
    Who, when in Englifh donjon bound,
Of Joan Beaufort's charms did fing.
    And fweet the captive monarch's found.
An ancient fpear may here be feen;
    A weighty lance hangs on the wall,
That had at Harlaw's battle been;
Here, too, a maffive fhield is fhown;
    And here a trumpet, at whofe call
The ready vaffals' fteps were known.
The pictures cheer the gazer's eye;

Nor lefs the trophied ftatuary :
Of Venice polifhed marble, here
Ten mighty warriors' busts appear !

XIII.

' *Ruthven, if yet within my reach*
  You ere fhould chance to ftray,
Direful the leffon I will teach
  Thee, coward, of thy way !''
Such accents from fierce Ruthven broke,
Who fhelter'd by a fhaggy oak ;—
Reftlefs was his flender form ;
  Subdued he feem'd by gathering rage ;
Madden'd his brain beneath the ftorm
  Of growing fpleen he fought to wage
On William Graham : he call'd Hell's aid,
And loud a dreadful oath he made !
Then ftared around ;—treach'rous his eye
  Hollow'd his pale, death-fpeaking cheek ;
Low was his forehead ; and his cry
  Rough in extreme ; his body weak,
  Though built on ample limbs ; his talk
Was all of felf : the country knew
His actions, and difdain'd them too !
He refted in anxiety,
While mufing paff'd our hero by ;

And as he lay the oak beneath,
Eager he caught each paffing breath ;
And as he heard his uncouth name,
Flafh'd from his eye the ireful flame.
" *Revenge on me !*" he groaning cried,
Turning his reftlefs form afide.
And ftill more angry turn'd his cry.
" Thanks for your boldnefs : I fhall try
The iffue of a future day,
And thus the challenge fhall repay !
' *Revenge on me !*' that thought is vain !
   I've the advantage—odds are mine ;
Nor, crefted youth, fhall I refrain
   To try thy father weak in time—
That he my ftory lifts is plain !
Graham, I have injured thee before,
And Ruthven vengeance feeks once more !
Then fpeed thee, pioneer of forrow !
O ! hafte thee, over-welcome morrow !
Then fhall the furies of my foul
Vent all my paffion at thy knoll,
Craighall !—That ruler of his heart,
   Mary Montgomery, mine fhould be ;
And fubtle was the unworthy art
   Made her eftrange her love from me.
'Tis this that makes me ever fad—

And lefs hath driven another mad :
'Tis this that robs me of my reft.
Was ever mortal fo oppreft ?
Depend, a day of reck'ning's near,
When gilded juftice fhall appear.
O hafte thee, time !. to-morrow come !
I long to fee what may be done."
Thus faid, he took the rugged road :
    A lonely houfe appear'd in fight—
Defigning Ruthven's lone abode.
    How picturefque in moonlight night !
'Twas heathery roof'd : the fwelling rains
Which deluge the adjacent plains
Befpoke deftruction :—fuch a fcene
Is feldom fancied in a dream.

XIV.

On Ocean's front the purple ray
Of dawn foretells approaching day :
Still higher rides the folar beam,
    Drinking the dewdrop from the fields ;
    And now each airy minftrel yields
    Libation of untutor'd fong,
    Heard all the dells and crags among.
And here the peafant may be feen
    Watching his herd upon the plain ;

Heard is the pointed fickle's noife,
   Falls to the ground the yellow grain.
Many the other welcome joys
That morning's radiant blufh imparts ;
Vig'rous from fleep Creation ftarts.

XV.

How beautiful the garden's bloom,
   Rounding the lofty manfion s fide :
The tulip and the lily's plume
   Welcome the rofe's ruddy pride ;
Lordly the venerable oaks
   That overlook the circled lakes,
Where oft the oarfman's fplafhing ftrokes
   The foft repofe of evening breaks.
Still farther, by the avenue,
Here may the veering optics view
   A pleafant, bubbling fountain play ;
Behold a miniature cafcade,
Which art for ornament hath made.
Yonder an artificial den
Attracts the wondering ftranger's ken ;
   And there arife the ruins grey
Of Abbey, where mafs oft was faid,
And pray'rs for Craighall's heroes made.
Here oft the aged and the poor

Rejoiced at monkifh charity ;
And here the ever open door
A refuge to the wanderer gave,—
To bleeding knight and warrior brave !
　　Here too, mayhap, our annals lay,
When ignorance unblufhing reign'd,
And credulity its hold maintain'd !

XVI.

Away a hunting party rode
　　From Craighall to the diftant moor—
Away by Ruthven's lone abode
　　Went Henry and his comrades four.
He watch'd the brave knight paffing by
　　(For William was not there),
And bitter, galling was the cry
　　That ftung the father's ear !
Immediately his choler rofe,
　　And inftantly he fwore,
That ne'er a fon, nor one of his,
　　Should fpeak Montgomery more !
" What !" as he foam'd, " my darling boy
Become the mate of fuch a toy !
The heir of all my lands, fhall he
Be knit and kneel to poverty !
O that my high ambition ftirr'd

His breaſt, and he had never err'd !
Perhaps a channel I may find
T" oppoſe the current of his mind.
I, who have climb'd the topmaſt high
When tempeſts wild diſturb'd the ſky—
I, who beheld the raving breeze
Raiſe every turmoil on the ſeas—
I who, adventurous, kept the right
Of powerful Blake in deſp'rate fight—
I, favour'd by nobility
And all the friends of liberty,—
Survey the actions of my ſon,
And wonder at his heart thus won !
This night my feelings I'll explode—
Witneſs my oath, Almighty God !

XVII.

He pauſed ; but heavier anger came
On the enraged Sir Henry Graham.
As when intoxication fills
The muddy brain, anon it reels ;
Such aſpect the old ſeaman wore,
From all the floods of grief he bore !
The ſun his weſtern courſe hath made,
For daylight now begins to fade—
Fades in the twilight's borrow'd hue,

And finks in the noƈturnal blue.
The fport is o'er; the hunters' tread
On Craighall's avenues are heard :
Known is the clamour in the court—
The clamorous boaft of endless fport.
But ah ! the fea-knight's meafured tone
Nor boaft had either liftener known;
Still kept his mind this deep dismay—
Thoughts of his fon on's fpirits prey.

XVIII.

To Gayford turn. . The mother broke
An hour of filence; thus fhe fpoke :
" O Mary dear, laft night I dream'd,
And ftrange indeed the vifion feem'd ;
Such horrors never croff'd my brain
Since Bothwell faw thy father flain !
Thy father—ah ! that gentle friend—
That model of a feeling mind !
No, fince I my dear hufband loft,
Like fcenes my fancy hath not croff'd :
And fhall I all the forms name ?
No ; better I conceal the fame.
Suffice, my daughter, they forbode
  And fhadow ills that we muft bear.
Oh ! ever Sorrow's dreary load

Crufhing our houfe, feems to appear !
Then, Mary, ftay thee for the night,
I fear to lend thee from my fight.
Stay, daughter, ftay—a mother's pray'r,
Perchance a faithful mother's tear,
Shall keep my cherifh'd daughter here !"

XIX.

" Ceafe, mother, with thy terrors ; ftill
Above them all is Mary's will.
Such might the unletter'd villain fway—
The villain born but to obey ;
But ne'er fhall education give
    To augur'd tales attention—Nay !
Enough they in the fhadow live—
    Enough they vanifh in the day.
    For fuch, O mother, fhall I ftay,
While William waits me to receive ?
    Already he is on his way—
Already, mother, it is eve.
" Vain, daughter, all thy reafoning yet.
    Can what is rooted in the mind
By the fharp fting of furrowing fate—
    Fate form'd too well fuch thoughts to bind—
Be thus, my daughter, torn afunder,
Even although tales of wonder ?

Say not I try thy loves to fever;
Far from my warmeſt wiſh—O never!
Admired the youth; his equal none.
   Yet pray, remember what I ſaid,—
Mayhap, before to-morrow come,
My old, my weather-worn eyes
Shall anguiſh vent by many ſighs:
   Remember this, beloved maid!

XX.

Here now with true parental love
The ſofter paſſions nobly ſtrove:
" I gave my word; that word, I trow,
Seems to me ſolemn as a vow."
Then went ſhe from the cottage ſide,
   And ſharply gain'd the trysting mount;
Here Mary, with becoming pride,
   Ruſh'd to her William's arms as wont.
A gloom acroſs his mind doth ride,
   Which borrow'd franknefs ſtrives to hide—
Ah vain! " Fly, Mary!—let us fly,
   The truth no longer I'll conceal:
Diſtreſſing was my father's cry,
   It did his anger ſtern reveal;
He rudely to my ſtudy came
   Two hours ago—downcaſt I left;

His threat'ning words I cannot name,
  Indeed he feem'd of fenfe bereft.

XXI.

Now, bent on wrong within the wood,
The diabolic Ruthven ftood!
A frenzy feized his frantic brain,
And poignant furely was the pain!
Woe to the man who boldly flies
Within his reach—the intruder dies!
And to himfelf, in angry mood,
He fpoke of vengeance and of blood!
" Now fhall Refentment fpread its thorns,
And, hydra-like, difplay its forms;
And now fhall Vengeance triumph here,
And glory that my foe is near!
Shall injured Love her wrongs difplay,
And o'er her trophy fmile fhe may;
Keen burns in me undying rage—
O! that I could him now engage!
Montgomery, what was love before
  Now flames in me as deadly hate;
Depend that I fhall clear the fcore,
  And rob thee of thy proffer'd mate!"

XXII.

Fail'd he in fearch of youthful Graham,
And nearer to the manfion came;
Rufh'd from the hall an aged man,
Who paff'd in anxious hafte the lawn—
  Prepared the defperate Ruthven now
To execute his bloody plan,
  And thus fulfil his demon vow;
Nor could his eye diftinguifh who
Towards the weft fo quickly drew—
Perhaps the darknefs of the night
Excufed the fiery Ruthven's fight.
He thought that William here fhould pafs.
Prepared his firelock—ready now, alas!
He aim'd a fure, a deadly wound,
Stretch'd Henry Graham upon the ground.
He cried for help—that help was near,
For William and the guefts appear!
They heard the noife: dread Ruthven fled,
And foon his diftant hamlet made—
Boafting that William Graham had met
An awful and unlook'd for fate.
Sir Henry heard his murderer named,
The fame who had his fon defamed:
" William," the dying feaman cried,

And, as the gen'rous youth he eyed—
" Forgive, forgive," he mutter'd low,
  The blood ftill gufhing from his heart—
" Forgive," again he faid; and lo !
  In this laft fit did life depart.

XXIII.

Scarce need we tell that juftice fought,
And to its bar fierce Ruthven brought :
A murderer's forfeit foon he paid—
Was forth unto the fcaffold led !
The country gloried in his fall,
His hated race was fcorn'd by all;
Nor need we fay that William made
A wife of Gayford's blooming maid !

The Pirate.

TEN weary years have roll'd away
Since red Culloden's dreadful day :
The gallant Cavalier* furvives,
And ftill at old Auchiries lives.
Stript of his family title, he
Lives lonely in obfcurity.
His lands have to a ftranger gone,
Unto the vaffalage unknown ;
Vain all the fearches for him made,
And all the offers for his head !
A dreary cell, fast by the wave,†
Awhile the warrior refuge gave ;

---

* Lord Forbes of Pitfligo.
† Cowfhaven, in the parifh of Aberdour, Aberdeenfhire.

But now his manly ftrength is gone,
But not the name his prowefs won!

   Ere Charles brave his standard raifed,
And fiery crofs through Badenoch blazed;
Secluded from the bufy world,
The foil a happy peafant turn'd—
Retainer of Pitfligo was,
Who favour'd much the Stuart caufe.
He rofe with morning to his toil,
And wealth him favour'd for a while;
His labour o'er, he loved to tell
What in his early days befell:
Deep verfed the peafant feemed to be
In Forbes genealogy!
The ftory of his fathers, too,
Each vifitant's attention drew.
Sometimes, in ruftic meafure ftrong,
Was heard an ancient rural fong;
The weather was a favourite theme,
And ftocks and harvefts he had feen.
The general topics of the times,
He at the smithy learn'd betimes;
In his unlearn'd companions' eyes
His firm opinions feem'd as wife.
How like a vaffal he obey'd

All the demands his Baron made!
At parifh church on Sunday he
Appeared with all his family;
A frugal and a virtuous wife
Cheerful made his ruftic life.
A gallant fon and blooming daughter,
Made him a truly happy father.
Of Helen much he loved to boaft,
Already was her name a toaft;
Many the fuitors that did come
Unto the jovial harvest-home.
The wily matron mother's art
Seems to have fway'd the daughter's heart.
Young Allan Forbes, the miller's fon,
Had oft to Ritchie's cottage come;
He fpent his winter evenings there,
Courting the young, the charming fair.
The focial glafs was handed round,
And Forbes was a votary found.
Ritchie was affable and free,
And kept his own distillery;
The many arts the excife tried,
The cunning farmer all defied!

In Helen's breaft the flame of love,
Delight for ftrapping Allan wove!

The youthful pair tryſts often ſet,
And near the ſhore the lovers met.
Along the ſandy beach they roved,
For Allan early ocean loved—
Admired the brave and gallant men
Who venturous plough'd the troubled main—
Columbus' life had thus inſpired,
And all his youthful ardour fired:
The ſtory of bold Gama, too,
The penetrating Forbes knew;
And from great Cabot he had learn'd
How wealth and honour might be earn'd.

A pleaſant picture this, till war
Did all theſe early pleaſures mar.
With grief ſtamp'd on his open face,
The youth his Helen did embrace;
The tears ſtood watery in his eyes,
At length they melted into cries—
Simply he told that he muſt go,
And face the Hanoverian foe;
His Baron at Edina was,
There he ſupported Charles' cauſe;
"I glory, Helen, at the sound,
In battle-field is honour found;
And yet I mourn I this muſt tell,

And bid thee, loved one, fad farewell!"
Pale now the charming maid appears,
Her beauteous cheeks are wet with tears—
Enough ftern manhood this to bend,
And make the female heart his friend!
A flow reply the maiden made :
She told her ftalwart brother had
Been alfo fummon'd.   Much fhe fear'd
That he, a brother much endear'd,
From his fuperior boldnefs might
Fall in the expected bloody fight.
She fear'd her Allan's fafety too—
Pain'd much her heart that word, " adieu ;"
He prefs'd her ruby lips—her hand
He circled with a filver band ;
Twice feven fparkling cairngorms,
The filver bracelet's fide adorns !
Pledging to meet again, they fever—
Would fortune blefs the loved and lover

The youth at Prestonpans fought well,
As Scotland's ftirring annals tell ;
In England was his bravery known,
And gallant he at Falkirk fhone !
'Twas here his Helen's brother met
A worthy Scottifh soldier's fate.

The princely Charles' active eye
Beheld the valiant peasant die—
The prince of active Forbes heard,
And named him of his body-guard.

Dreadful Culloden has been fought,
And Allan Forbes a refuge fought.

Still fwell'd his heart with Highland pride,
Difgrace the youth could not abide;
He fwore he ne'er return would home
Till fame or fortune he had won!
The greatest hazard he would try,
For nought could daunt his bravery.
From fearch of piercing Cumberland
He with a small but faithful band
Escaped: they venturous fought the fea,
And there difplay'd their gallantry.

Ten times the circling earth had run
Around that central orb the fun.
The braveft of Pitfligo's men
Had in this bloody war been flain.
The land of mirth and pleafure now
Nought but adverfity could fhew.
The peafant's ftamp of wretchednefs

Befpoke a growing wildernefs.
Deēp melancholy Ritchie fway'd,
Damp'd was the mother and the maid—
That ftalwart youth, his father's pride
And mother's hope, for ever fled!
And, with a feeling heart, he grieves
The lofs of many relatives.
Deep the laments for Allan made,
The gallant youth they fancied dead—
" What caufe have we to ftruggle here
Sever'd from all that makes life dear?"
The deep defponding Ritchie faid :
His fpoufe's tears the fadnefs fed—
" One by one my friends have gone ;
Unfriended, I am left alone !
Our mighty lord no more retains
An inch of all his native plains.
He was a landlord true and kind,
And dignified his noble mind !
How different his fucceffors : they
Seem Mammon only to obey.
And let us, ere our all be gone,
And ere our fading ftrength is done,
O'er wide Atlantic feek a home.
There is my elder brother known—
There priftine pleafures may awake,

And happy yet an old man make;
There may our virtuous daughter gain
The hand of fome kind, gen'rous fwain.
In this event, would forrow ceafe—
Would forrow find its vent in peace.
Your motherly advice I afk,
To aid me in this weighty task."
The frugal fpoufe then made reply :
" Not that I have no tender tie
Wifh I to leave the Scottifh foil,
And bid farewell to Britain's ifle,
But that I fee approaching faft
Poverty's degrading blast :
An increased rent we cannot pay,
Nor tyrant landlord fhall obey ; ,
Then let us from such vortex fteer,
While yet our funds can keep us clear.
Your brother's ftation is advanced,
His wealth and greatnefs much enhanced—
I think, with justice, we may leave,
Nor at our quick departure grieve."

The daughter next gave her confent—
Well was her juft opinion meant :
She fancied that her Allan yet
Might on Virginian foil be met.

c

Many the offers fhe had fpurn'd,
For sure her trueft, earlieft love yet burn d;
Deep rooted in her bofom, fhe
Could not conceal its ardency.

Already hath the veffel fail'd,
For favouring winds the while prevail d.
Twice twenty emigrants fhe bore,
Who look'd for rich Virginia's fhore.
Gently the wind begins to rife,
When, lo! a barque the captain eyes:
She nears, alas! a pirate this!—
" A pirate, feamen, makes for us!
Spread, failors, fpread thy every fail—
Stretch all thy canvafs to the gale!   ·
There yet is hope, our fhip is fleet,
And may the pirate's aim defeat."
Immediately this toil is o'er,
The veffel fcuds the winds before;
The emigrants, with tremor fraught,
Already fancied they were caught—
That they 'd be made the pirate's flaves,
Or meet with death in ocean's waves.
All thoughts of future wealth have fled,
Of cherish'd life all are afraid!
Old Ritchie's and his daughter's yells

The terrors of each mind betells;
The captain faw their fpirits fade,
And thus a fhort addrefs he made:
" Difpel thy fears, for never yet
So fleet a veffel have I met
As that which thee conveys—full oft
Have I Algerian corfair left;
Or, if the worft muft fhortly come,
Let every man to weapon run,
For all have fomething now to lofe;
To yield, I know, no man will choofe.
What are thefe pirates?—They are men,
In this you equal are to them;
Ours the defence, and boldly, too,
We'll fhow the mettle of the crew!"

All terrors now began to fly,
Hope brighten'd up each fading eye;
Already fome began to boaft
Of how they would maintain their poft.
Aloft his eyes the captain rears,
For too much fail his veffel bears.
Alas! now one top-gallant mast bends—
It breaks, and in the brine defcends;
The topfail, too, is borne away,
It alfo greets the dafhing fpray.

Wonted bravery forfakes
The crew; on them the pirate makes.
Two hundred yards hath he to run,
Another treafure may be won!
" Yield!" the gallant rover cried—
To this the captain ne'er replied.
Gently the wind begins to fade—
Still on the fhip the corsair made.
Increased the mafter pirate's ire,
He on the fhip begins to fire;
He gains her fide—this doth afford
His brother pirates time to board.
He alfo leaps into the fhip,
Afks boldly where the treafures fleep.
The captain this difdain'd to tell,
And in the defp'rate ftruggle fell.
With dirks the failors vengeance fought—
With knives the emigrants now fought.
The pirates 'gan to ftrip the dead,
And every fearch for plunder made.
The females they difdain'd to flay,
But tore their jewels bright away.
The mafter pirate boldly fought
The treafures Helen fair had got;
He feized her firmly by the hand—
Call'd loudly to his men to ftand!

All of a fudden he did ftart—
Tender the thoughts that pierced her heart :
The bracelet which, ten years before,
He Helen gave, the maid ftill wore !
The fofter paffions now awoke,
And filence thus the pirate broke :
Helen, entranced, full wond'rous stared,
And fancied fhe her Allan heard !
"Thrice charming Helen !—ah ! that I
Am father of this butchery !
Long years of fad defpondency
Have made me relifh piracy :
Wilt thou my feelings now forgive,
And, long as Allan Forbes fhall live,
You find fhall him an alter'd man—
A faithful, true companion.
Here on this bloody deck you fee
Many who fought for Charles with me.
The bravest from Pitfligo are,
All famed in ' Forty-five's ' dread war.
My love is pure as heaven yet,
And Helen's like I never met ;
Let memory of the paft depart,
And take me, Helen, to thy heart."

Cheer'd and downcaft was fhe by turns,

For gathering-love and forrow burns!
The father and the mother knew
The event, and near the pirate drew.
Both were inclined to overlook
The paft: Allan his courfe forfook!
A vow to this effect he made,
And generofity difplay'd!
He went and told each bold compeer;
Advifed the end of this career!
To this they nobly all agreed,
And of their many crimes were freed.
The emigrants the oblivion gave,
Now all admired the pirates brave;
In this the failors alfo joined—
True friendfhip hath both crews combined.
The pirate treafures were convey'd,
And fafely in this veffel laid;
The pirate fhip they allow'd to ride
Without a helmfman on the tide!

The crews and emigrants foon found
A home on rich Virginia's ground.

Strathaven Castle.

I.

HE fnowfalls of winter had mantled the ground,
    And fwell'd into torrents Pomillon's dark bed;
At diftance is heard the loud Kype's brawling found,
    As over the cafcade its waters are led;
Roufed is the wild Aven, fo claffic in fong,
    So varied in themes all exciting of old;
Now fhorn of their herbage the trees that along
    Its lofty banks frown on the precipice bold;
And, lo! in the diftance, gleams Loudoun's round hill,
And plays at its bafe the Irvine's ftretch'd rill.

II.

Here the eagles of Rome were outfpread to the fkies,
    When the laurel'd Agricola fwept our loved Ifle:

Now gory the braveſt of Caledon lies,
    For the fair ſun of fortune has left them the while !
Here the Knights of the Temple, from Aſia return'd,
    The champions who figured in Turkiſh cruſade,
While the ſtrength and the pride of the Ottoman burn'd;
    In the cauſe of the croſs and religion they bled,
And the temple of Judah, now faded, maintain'd,—
Untenured the lordſhip of Darvel obtain'd.

III.

Here Wallace the mighty met Scotland's proud foes ;
    With his ſmall faithful body the Engliſh he foil'd ;
For ſeemly gigantic his proweſs aroſe !
    See there, to his mem'ry, a cairn is piled.
Here Pembroke met Bruce with the rude mountaineers ;
    The valley the hoſt of great Edward beheld.
How deadly the pierce of the ſharp Scottiſh ſpears,
    For Robert triumphant rides firſt on the field.
Here the rude oaks of Caledon ſhelter'd her deer,
And ſtill on the marſhes their huge trunks appear.

IV.

Here, elated with victory, fierce Balfour high ſtood,
    Deem'd Covenant's hero and Preſbyter's friend ;
And ſtill here the offspring of gentleſt blood
    On each anniverſary devotions forth ſend

To the great God of battles, who favour'd the caufe
  For which our loved fathers in myriads fell.
On the traveller's keen eye an obelifk draws,
  Which fimply records on its fide the war tale.
In priftine fimplicity the peafant ftill dwells,
And boafts of his Scotland, her moors and her hills.

V.

Turn now to Pomillon, on whofe weftern edge
  The huge Gothic pile of Strathaven is feen ;
But the full weight of years and the elements' rage
  Have changed to a fragment what fortrefs had been.
'Twas Murdoch the Regent that reared the walls,
  And doughty black Douglas held here princely fway.
The vaffals of Clydefdale awoke at his call,
  And follow'd the high Earl to battle or fray.
Ah ! woe to the foe who beheld his advance,
  For fubjection or ruin gleam'd bright on his lance !

VI.

When the Douglas rebellion was crufh'd by his fire,
  When attainted his titles and wide-circled fields,
And extinguifh'd the fpark of his anceftors' fire—
  How oft unto juftice ambition thus yields !—
To Stewart the rich lordfhip of Aven was given,
  With its caftle, fo oft by the valiant affail'd,

The valiant fo oft from its ample front driven;
   By its fide each retainer his rude hamlet held.
Activity triumphs; the fhuttle and loom,
And high found of commerce, betoken the town.

VII.

The fair Margaret Stewart in a room lonely fat,
   When enter'd her uncle, great Avendale's lord:
High fhone his red count'nance with bright hope elate;
   Sufpenfe for the while feem'd to hang on his word.
" What! once cherifh'd Margaret," he nervoufly faid;
   " Wilt thou yet refufe the bold Baron of Clyde?
Lord Nethan, who long to me vifits hath made:
   He is gen'rous and brave; his dominions are wide;
His vaffals are many—all valiant in fight:
This, Margaret, he offers—he'll wed thee to-night."

VIII.

" What! wed me to-night! this is furely a dream.
   What! wed me to-night! to the Baron I hate!
No! never, my uncle! this madnefs doth feem,
   For never fhall I with that rude warrior mate.
Full oft hath he tried my foft paffions to fway;
   His conduct's repulfive indeed to my heart.
Well knows he my mind: then, idea, away;
   Let the thought of fuch union for ever depart,

For true is the flight my foft paffions now take—
To another, my uncle, my amours I make."

IX.

" Another, my niece! O avaunt fuch a thought!
For to-night the great Baron of Nethan comes here.
Rejoice, O my Margaret, he falls to thy lot.
Proceed to thy chamber, and gaily appear
In robes of the brighteft that Scotland can fhow;
And the lands of Drumclog I fhall give as thy dower.
Already the ladies affemble; and lo!
Great Nethan comes quickly. O bleffed the hour
When the Abbot of Paifley fhall ftand forth in pride,
And hail thee, fweet Margaret, as Lord Nethan's bride!"

X.

" Never, never, alas!—I have fworn it—O never!
My heart is another's, and no longer my own.
My uncle, 't were vain me from Walter to fever;
More courteous and kind than he never was known."
Away went the Baron in forrowful mood;
The ftings that him tortured no pen can exprefs;
Suffice that his brow told a gathering of blood,
And forrow and anger feem'd ftamp'd on his face.
" Another! how vain! fhall he ftand in the path—
A vaffal of mine—when my word brings him death?"

XI.

" What though my fquire, Walter Cochrane, is bold,
  And forth on the red field triumphant did ride,
When the death-fpeaking weapons were vig'roufly
    roll'd,
  And thoufands rejoiced in the downfall of Boyd;
Or when civil war dark deftruction had fpread,
  And the blood of the nobleft lay fwimming around;
Or when Scotland's high monarch fummon'd my aid,
  Firft he through the moors to Linlithgow did bound:
Of all my great vaff'lage, he's greateft by far—
The gentleft in peace, and the braveft in war!

XII.

" But my word to Lord Nethan th' act juftifies,
  For the heart and the thoughts of the vaffal are mine;
Nor the wailing of women, nor all his loud cries,
  Can leffen the deed that muft fhortly be done;
For ne'er fhall the blood of Aven's chiefs proud
  In the veins of a vaffal contaminate run!
Never yet unto meannefs a Stewart hath bow'd,
  And nought but the nobleft a Stewart hath won—
A Stewart now fits upon Fergus' high throne,
And we of a branch of this family are come."

XIII.

Away went the Baron; a villain obtain'd,
 Inured to fell hardſhips, at death ſeem'd to ſmile;
The name of a murderer his deeds him obtain'd;
 Long'd he for the blood of young Walter the while;
The Baron's ſtill whiſper high tranſport him gave,
 And the words of reward ſounded well in his ear.
Sought he for colleague a like daſtard knave;
 And now the dark demons as loitering appear—
The gallant Squire, thoughtleſs, ſtill paced the hall floor,
When heavy the ſteps that he heard at the door.

XIV.

Ruſh'd now to the hall the wild dealers in blood,
 Whoſe looks ſanction'd ſome deſp'rate act of revenge.
As caught by ſurpriſe the brave Walter now ſtood,
 Suſpicious, alas! of ſome heart-rending change.
They bore him away to a dark, frowning cell;
 Ah! vain was the ſtruggle for liberty tried.
Here the captive doth pine, and deſpondency dwell,
 And here are the words of confeſſor denied;
When the weapons of death the brave Cochrane here
  eyed,
 Oft, oft for his Margaret he bitterly ſigh'd.

XV.

" Tyrannic, the Baron, o'erlooking my worth,
　　Who hired thefe affaffins to th' act that fhall ftain
(For the world and freedom fhall herald it forth)
　　And with infamy brand the Lord Avendale's name.
Not even the fierce favage of African wild,
　　Nor unbridled Tartar of ravaging horde
Of great Tamerlane, who fair Afia defpoil'd,
　　Could thus my fidelity unexampled reward !
Can this be the fumma—this the price of my faith—
A cruel, ignominious, and degrading death !

XVI.

" Unmerited death ! and denied e'en the fight
　　Of th' accufer whofe name I fo boldly maintain'd ;
For him I have conquer'd and flain many wight,
　　In fierce Scottifh war and in Border fray famed ;
Of the acts unapprifed for which I muft die.
　　My dear blooming Margaret !—how bleffed the
　　　　found !—
For one lone embrace, and one only, I figh ;
　　For thee, oh my eyeballs are turn'd around ;
But turn'd all in vain ; that our love muft expire
Ere it has expanded its pure virgin fire !

XVII.

" Can this be for love, for thou firft loved me :
   If so, unto death I would willingly bend.
Could I think, my dear Margaret, it fhelter would thee,
   My head—O ! for thee—I had quickly extend !
I would willingly clofe the affairs of this life,
   And long for the future of good and of blifs.
Oh ! happy, when Death fets his feal on the ftrife,
   And clofes mortality, woe, and diftrefs !
We meet fhall again after few fleeting years,
When the bright joys of heaven fhall have dried all thy
      tears !

XVIII.

A huge fpear is raifed, 'tis all rufty with gore—
   The dreadful affaffins feem'd to fmile at the fight :
Marble the hue that young Walter now wore,
   While feemly gigantic he fummon'd his might.
The name of the murderer is call'd in the hall,
   And the found of the Baron has reach'd his sharp ear,
Prepared the dark villain to anfwer the call,
   He hands to his colleague the knife and the fpear,
Who ftruck the young Cochrane—his vigorous arm
Defended his breaft, and repulfed the alarm !

XIX.

The fpear Walter feized from the wavering hand
    Of the defp'rate affaffin, and him ftretch'd at his foot ;
And now, as avenger, our hero doth ftand—
    His once threat'ning en'my is filent and mute.
Such deeds of defpair due defpatch doth require—
    The heart of the murd'rer is fever'd in two :
Our hero, triumphant, beholds him expire,
    Then quick as the wing'd fheet of lightning he flew,
And with one well laid on Vulcanian ftroke,
The bars of the old grated window he broke !

XX.

He look'd o'er the wall, and prepared for the leap,
    Pomillon was noify, and favour'd his caufe :
But what though the mound was wild, rocky, and fteep,
    He ne'er for a moment of fuch thought could paufe.
He leapt, and in fafety the grafs gain'd below.
    The evening now told his approach on the fkies,
And the breezes of Boreas ftill hoarfely do blow :
    The rain falls in torrents—the melted fnow hies
To a channel : gay the affemblage that comes—
How ftalwart the knights, bright their daughters and
    sons !

XXI.

Lord Nethan arrived, and he walk'd near the cell
  So lately the fcene of this favage affray!
When the daftard who left on the noble lord fell—
  All of a fudden interrupted his way!
They knew not each other, for Darknefs had fpread
  His covering of fable within the rude walls.
Ah! little dreamt Crawford his colleague lay dead,—
  Now, alas! on the corpfe of that colleague he falls!
He feized the Lord Nethan, enraged, by the throat,
As the fpear by the fide of fierce Jackfon he fought!

XXII.

```
 *        *        *        *        *
     *        *        *        *
 *        *        *        *        *
     *        *        *        *
```

Fair Margaret, of young Walter's fafety afraid,
  Now hies to her chamber all lone in diftrefs—
How rending the cries that the fweet female made,
  For her tendereft ties fhe attempts to confefs!
She dreaded her uncle her Walter had found—
That he in the donjon lay fetter'd and bound.

D

XXIII.

" To fee him were heaven ! to arrange for our flight—
    For to him may all fecrets of Margaret be told !
Chill and unpleafant is the dark frofty night,
    That in camp pains the foldier, fo fearlefs and bold.
How welcome to him is the gay glance of morn—
    Such unto me is the fight of my Walter !
Since we parted full many the pains I have borne,
    With the fortitude—yes—of a High Steward's
      daughter.
O give me again the bleft object I love,
That I with my Walter by Aven may rove !

XXIV.

" Again, if that can be but hoped—oh ! again
    To think, my dear Walter, of cold feparation !
Down, down with the thought, for its import is vain,
    And pregnant to me with moft poignant vexation.
If my fierce uncle's ire can have robb'd thee of life,
    Sure thou with the feraphs art joyful in heaven !
No more curfed earth fhall behold me in ftrife,
    Since the power thee to follow, my Walter, is given.
But, oh ! if in donjon thou, loved one, fhould pine,
Depreffing the thoughts that muft ever be mine.

XXV.

" But I'll folve the doubt in a minute's fhort fpace,
　I 'll forward and eye the dark den's awful mouth,
And fee if my lover I yet may embrace,
　Or meet with fights horrid, unwelcome, uncouth."
Thus mufed the bright gem of the wild Aven vale,
　When a found, lo! like Walter's, caught her fharp
　　ear ;
That found was a lover's—a lover's fad wail ;
　'Twas the voice that the lady fo oft loved to hear !
She turn'd of a fudden—look'd over the fteep—
And there faw her Walter—for her he did weep !

XXVI.

The blood feem'd to gufh from his arm and cheek ;
　He tower'd his bright eyes, and his Margaret beheld—
He rofe : ah ! his limbs and his body were weak,
　But the bright flufh of joy o'er his fair features roll'd.
The lady, full joyful, now leapt in his arms—
　No feat, fure, too great for defpair or for love !
Her boldnefs the heart of the gallant fquire warms.
　To open her mind to her lover fhe ftrove—
She fpake, and her words were in favour of flight ;
Their caufe was fupported by darknefs of night !

XXVII.

With every luxury the tables were ſpread—
    The attendants were many, and rare to behold ;
At Strathaven before ſuch diſplay ne'er was made,
    The nobles were many, and valiant, and bold—
They came from the Clyde, from the Nethan, and Ayr ;
    And many the knights that in armour bright ſhone—
And many the ladies, all courteous and fair—
    To match blooming Margaret there ne'er yet was
      one !
Full long look'd the party for bridegroom and bride,
And loud for his niece the Lord Avendale cried.

XXVIII.

His echoes were vain, for his niece was not there ;
    Now crimſon the imprint of rage that he wore.
And where is Lord Nethan, the bridegroom ? oh! where
    Was like diſappointment ere witneſſ'd before !
Away to the donjon Lord Avendale ran—
    Diſtreſſing the ſcene that now ſteals on his eye ;
For Nethan lies here all ſickly and wan,
    And the meſſenger pale ſeems as hovering nigh !
The blood-ruſty weapon Lord Avendale found,
And the murd'rous vaſſal ſoon died of the wound.

XXIX.

Three years has the mighty Lord Avendale changed—
 At the Abbey of Paifley he penance hath paid;
He mourn'd for the lady he lately eftranged.
 Now many the friends that his clemency made—
Was loved by the great and the noble around—
 His vaffals long gloried to echo his praife;
The Church, in Lord Avendale, patron now found,
 And long to his mem'ry the monks fhouts did raife.
Thus cruelty mirror'd and heralded forth,
Is often fubverted to kindnefs and worth!

XXX.

From the depth of the wound, and the forrows that prey'd
 On his mind, the rejected Lord Nethan foon died.
While Cochrane and Margaret to France were convey'd,
 And there by a father of Rouen were tied.
Rode Walter as knight with the famous French fire,
 And the Spaniard and German oft fhrunk from his
  fword.
Oh! oft has the minftrel, on heart-melting lyre,
 The young fquire of Aven and Margaret adored!
Many the Cochranes on Fame's roll that ftand,
And ftill their defcendants are great in that land!

Maffacre of Eigg.

[The following ballad is founded on a well-known hiftorical fact.]

EVERY chieftain of the Ifles
    Trembles at the princely name
Of Aliftair, the great M'Leod,
    Who nobly doth our homage claim!

Thus cried a bold and forward crew,
    Paffing rocky Eigg's rude coaft;
The fails are flapping in the wind,
    And on the waves the boat is toff'd.

A broken galley beats the furge,
    And human cries difturb the fcene:

" Methinks," the watchful helmſman ſpake,
  " Familiar, ſure, that voice did ſeem.

" Familiar, yes !"—they lower'd the ſails,
  The weather-beaten boatmen row'd :
And to that galley chain'd they found
  Three followers of the ſtern M'Leod.

" M'Leod ! that inſult on our name !
  Revenge ! revenge !" the ſailors cry :
" The authors of this bloody work
  By ſome ignoble death ſhall die.

" But whence the cauſe ?" the boatman aſks—
  " What forced the cowards to this deed ?
How ſweet is vengeance on a foe !
  We love to ſee our foemen bleed."

Lies form'd but to conceal the truth,
  The fierce, inhuman captives framed ;
The horrors of the picture, ſure,
  Are too degrading to be named !

The captives inſtant refuge found :
  " Our valiant chief ſhall learn this tale,"

Was echo'd by the incenſed crew
   That for Dunvegan's tower ſet ſail.

Clanranald's Iſles they quickly clear,
   And the bleak weſtern ſhore of Skye;
And, paſſing through the Tollart's ſwell,
   The ancient Daniſh tower draws nigh.

Dunvegan's huge romantic pile,
   The work of Scandinavian hands,
Was rear'd when Eric braved the world,
   And fought the Pict and Saxon bands.

Here ſhone in arms the brave M'Leod,
   Attended by his faithful bard—
Whoſe ſongs in honour of the clan
   So oft its warlike members heard.

Full oft the piper's martial notes
   Ring in the patriarchal hall;
The ſquire and gillie here attend,
   And liſt the mountain chieftain's call.

Unmatch'd for hoſpitality
   Is he, ſprung from great Rory More;

Now round he hands the mighty cup
   That Somerled had quaff'd of yore.

The captives drown the notes of joy,
   How melancholy their complaint!
The lift'ning father of the clan
   Thus gave his growing paffion vent :—

" Go, flaughter now the mountain goat,
   And burn the crofs of hazel-wood—
Extinguifh then the rifing flame,
   In the victim's reeking blood.

" Send forth this fignal of alarm,
   To roufe the warlike men of Skye ;
For by the fword of ftern M'Leod
   Clanranald's favage tribe fhall die !''

An hundred hardy Celts appear'd
   Dunvegan's ample front before ;
Rejoiced each plaided warrior,
   Brandifhing his dark claymore.

" Go, man the boats," the chieftain faid,
   " And I the noble pomp fhall fwell ;''

Ten monſtrous galleys cut the tide,
 And for Eigg's fated iſland ſail.

Fated, alas! the Iſleſmen learn
 The approach of their terrific foe—
" O how ſhall we this force reſiſt?
 Unaided, how repel the blow?

" Our daughters raviſh'd in our ſight
 By this fierce avenging race;
'Twas ours, alas! to witneſs, too,
 Augmented ſcenes of deep diſgrace.

" O let us to the cavern fly,
 And there evade ſtern Creloch's wrath,
For ſure that haughty Gael has fix'd
 On ſome unwelcome game of death."

The counſell'd natives ſwiftly ruſh'd
 Unto the vaſt, the ample cave;
Another rough and hollow'd rock
 Three aged warriors refuge gave.

M'Leod arrived: deſcending ſnows
 Mantled Scoor Rigg's lofty brow—

Increaſed the fury of that chief,
   In abſence of his timid foe.

Thrice paced his men the unhappy Iſle—
   The muddy huts aſcend in flames;
The work of plunder is complete,
   But ſlaughter ſtill the chieftain aims.

Two days he ſearch'd for Francis Cave—
   Two days he ſearch'd, but all in vain!
Prepared the morning of the third
   To ſeek Dunvegan's tower again.

Uneaſy in the dreary den
   The iſlanders ſent forth a ſpy,
And from a galley's deck his form
   Caught a ſharp ſeaman's glancing eye.

Fruitleſs the attempts M'Donald made,
   His treach'rous footprints to conceal.
Ah, fatal! for the trodden ſnow
   Doth the vaſt cavern's front reveal.

Rejoiced M'Leod: at the den's mouth
   He aſk'd the daſtards who had chain'd

And ſent his followers to the ſea,—
   If ſuch within its bounds remain'd ?

Proud of their hold, the anſwer " No "
   Was ſyllabled by every tongue—
" We are the injured," from the cave,
   Loud as M'Donald's war cry rung.

Glowing with hate the chieftain ſpoke—
   " Divert the ſilvery ſtream which flows
By the cave's mouth, that I may lave
   On this proud race relentleſs woes."

'Tis done : bared is the heathery Iſle
   Of heath to miniſter revenge—
Choked the den's mouth—now lit the fire,
   And ſmoke doth through the cavern range.

Still burns the proud avenger's fire—
   The Iſleſmen's dying agonies
High flowing pleaſure did afford
   To their atteſted enemies.

Alas ! that hiſtory ſhould record
   This ſhocking, dark, barbarian tale—
That ſuch atrocity ſhould lower
   Our eſtimation of the Gael !

Finis.

www.ingramcontent.com/pod-product-compliance
Lightning Source LLC
Chambersburg PA
CBHW021226260626
47172CB00002B/625